Wake Up!

Written by Drew Jones

Illustrated by Andrew Hopgood

"Let's watch the sunrise
in the morning," said Sam.

Dad set the alarm clock.

Soon Sam was asleep.

Mandy was asleep.

Dad was asleep.

Tick, tock. Tick, tock.
Tick, tock... *Clunk.*
The clock stopped.

Sam was still asleep.
Mandy was still asleep.
Dad was still asleep.

Then Sam woke up.
He could hear birds singing.
But he couldn't hear
the clock!

"Wake up!" he shouted.
"The clock has stopped."

"Is it time to watch the sunrise?" asked Mandy.

"Yes! We have to hurry!"
said Sam.

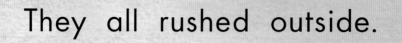

They all rushed outside.

14

"Look! The sun's coming up," said Dad.

"Wow!" said Sam.
"We were just in time."